A Love Like This

Written by
Skyler Houston

Illustrated by
Gaurav Bhatnagar

About the Author

Skyler Houston Willingham, or Skye as she is often referred, is originally from Philadelphia, Mississippi, but was raised in Athens, Georgia. She has always been passionate about writing and children. Skye enjoys traveling and trying new eateries. "A Love Like This" is the third book in its series.

This book belongs to

_____

Published & Copyright © 2021 by Skyler Houston
A Love Like This

Illustrations by ePublishingeXperts Art Studio
www.epublishingexperts.com
Edited by Dr. Carla Gray

This edition first published in 2021 by Skyler Houston
All rights reserved.

No part of this publication may be reproduced, distributed, or transmitted in any form or by any means, including photocopying, recording, or other electronic or mechanical methods, without the prior written permission from the author, except in the case of brief quotations embodied in reviews and certain other non-commercial uses permitted by copyright law.

Ordering information
Special discounts are available on quantity purchases by corporations, schools, libraries, charities, etc.

For information please email
authorskylerhouston@gmail.com
ISBN: 978-0-578-92382-6

Printed in United States

It is going to be a fun night! I am having a movie night with my sister, Jamie and my brother, Jake. Mommy and Daddy are going on a date tonight to celebrate their 25th Anniversary, so it will be just the three of us.

I like it when Daddy takes Mommy on dates.
It makes Mommy happy, so Daddy is happy too!

Daddy let me pick out flowers, so he can surprise Mommy. Mommy let me pick out her dress for tonight. Mommy loves yellow, so I picked out yellow flowers and a yellow dress! I cannot wait for Daddy to see Mommy in her new dress.

As Jamie, Jake, and I wait on Mommy and Daddy to head out for the evening, we prepare for our movie night. Jamie pops the popcorn. Jake sets up our movie on the television. "Hurry with the pillows and blankets, Jordan," Jake says excitedly.

I scurry to the living room with the pillows and blankets and plop down on the sofa. We get comfortable.

Mommy and Daddy make their way downstairs to the living room. Mommy looks pretty! Daddy looks nice too.

Daddy sneaks away to the kitchen to grab the flowers for Mommy.

Daddy gives Mommy the flowers.
Mommy is pleasantly surprised.
"These sunflowers are beautiful!
Thank you, Honey," beams Mommy.
She gives Daddy a big hug and
a kiss.

"You are welcome. Happy Anniversary, Sweetheart! You look beautiful tonight," exclaims Daddy. He carries Mommy's coat, and heads to the door.

"See you later, Kiddos! We love you," declares Daddy. "Happy Anniversary, Mommy and Daddy! We love you, too," we yell. Then we run to the door.

We give Mommy and Daddy hugs and kisses before they leave for their date.

Daddy opens the front door for Mommy. They walk out the door and head to the car.

Daddy opens the car door, and he gently helps Mommy get into her seat. He closes her door. Daddy walks briskly to the other side of the car, sits in his seat, and starts to drive away.

We stand in the doorway and wave until they are out of our sight. Gazing at the faint red glare from the rear lights of the car, I tell Jamie and Jake that I want a love like Mommy's and Daddy's when I grow up.

"Me too, Jordan," blurt both Jamie and Jake. "For now, let's get to this movie and popcorn," chuckles Jake.

CPSIA information can be obtained
at www.ICGtesting.com
Printed in the USA
BVHW021411030921
615987BV00017B/249